ER
SUT

Fun With Mo and Ella

By Tui T. Sutherland
Illustrated by Rose Mary Berlin

Library of Congress Cataloging-in-Publication Data is available.

ISBN 0-448-42638-2   A B C D E F G H I J

Grosset & Dunlap • New York

Happy Birthday, Mo and Ella!

Mo and Ella have the same birthday!

They like to make presents.
What will they make?

Mo has a great idea.

He will make a blanket for Ella!

Ella has a great idea.

She will make a hat for Mo!

Squeak squeak squeak!
Mo works hard.
Shhhhh…it's a secret!

Clomp Clomp Clomp!
Ella works hard.
Shhhhh…it's a secret!

They are done!

The presents are perfect!

Oops!
This blanket is too small for Ella.

Oops!
This hat is too big for Mo.

A scarf! It is perfect!

A bed! It is perfect!

Squeak squeak squeak!

Clomp Clomp Clomp!

Happy birthday, best friends!

A New Friend for Mo and Ella!

Mo and Ella are best friends.

Who is this?

Her name is Hippa.
She is a hippo.
She is loud.

Ella is big.
So is Hippa.

Ella likes to go
Clomp Clomp Clomp!
So does Hippa.

Mo is small.
He can not go
Clomp Clomp Clomp!

Ella and Hippa are friends.

Mo is sad.

Let's go swimming!

Ella looks for Mo.

Ella looks up.

Ella looks down.

No Mo.

Who will ride on my ear?

Who will go
squeak squeak squeak!
and make me smile?

Ella is sad.

Ella calls Mo.
SQUEAK SQUEAK SQUEAK!
she yells.

It is very funny.

There you are, Mo!

We can <u>all</u> go swimming!

Squeak squeak squeak!

Clomp Clomp Clomp!

Best friends forever!